May 2009    Great River Regional Library

W9-CPN-416

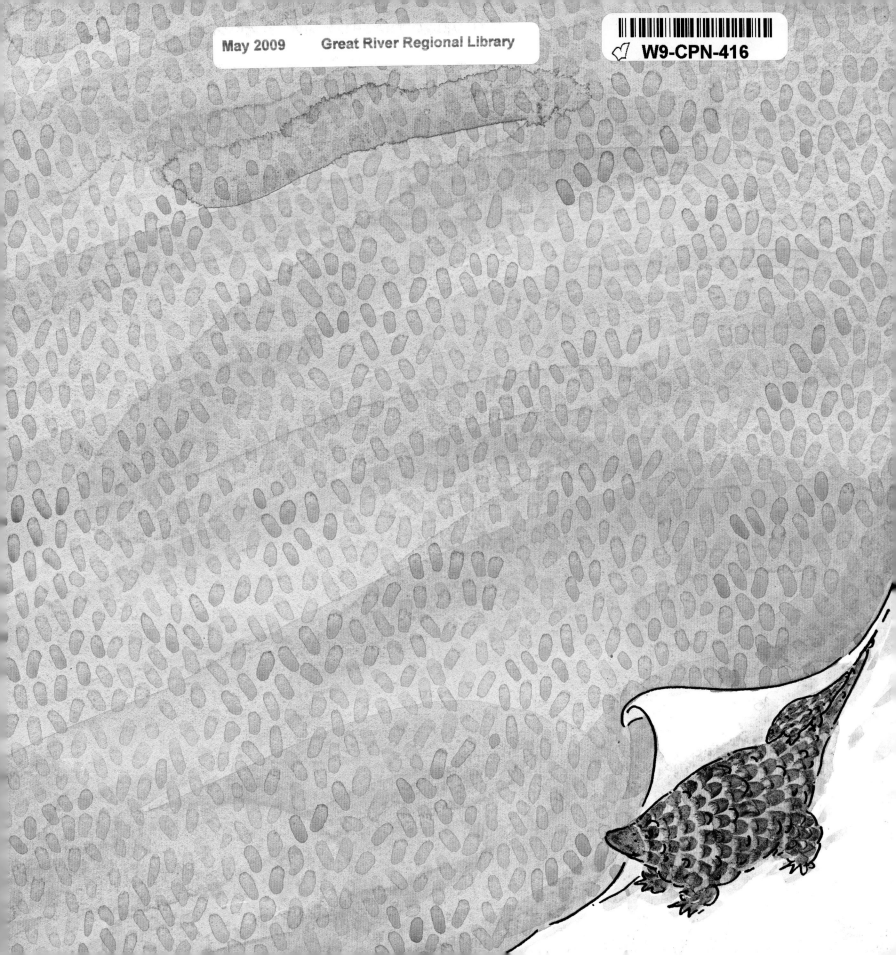

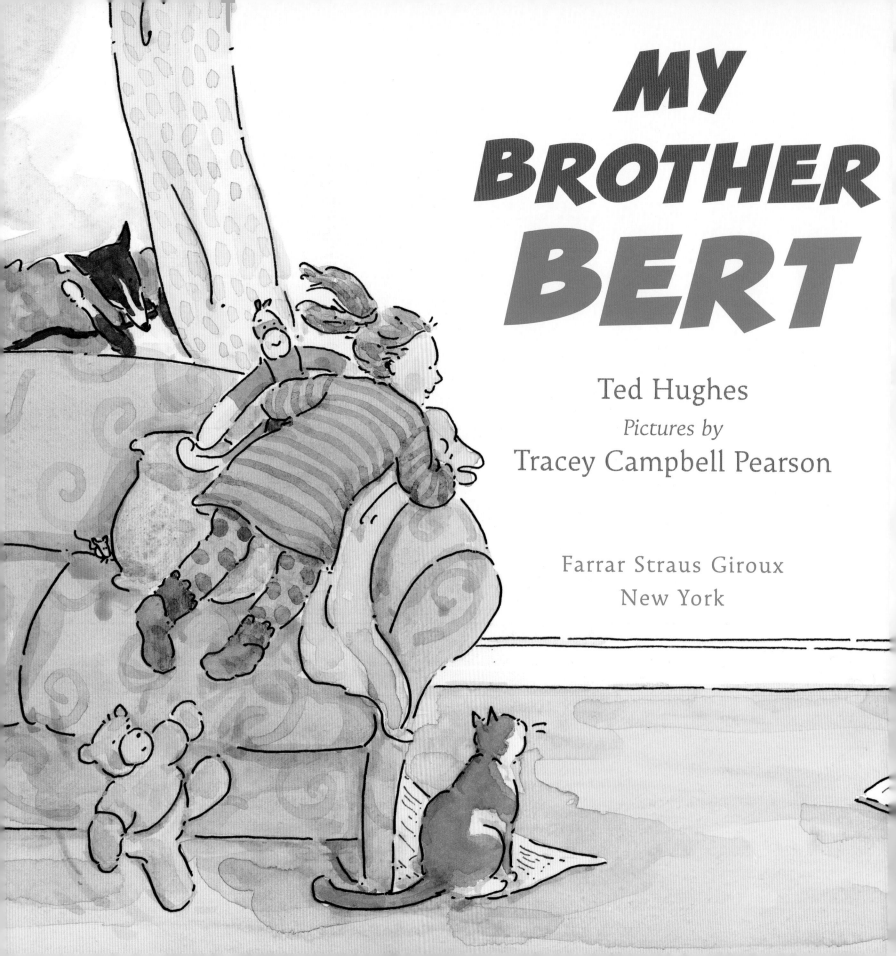

# MY BROTHER BERT

Ted Hughes

*Pictures by*
Tracey Campbell Pearson

Farrar Straus Giroux
New York

Pets are the Hobby of my brother Bert.
He used to go to school with a Mouse in his shirt.

His Hobby it grew, as some hobbies will,

And grew and GREW and GREW until—

Oh don't breathe a word, pretend you haven't heard.
A simply appalling thing has occurred—

The very thought makes me iller and iller:

Bert's brought home a gigantic Gorilla!

If you think that's really not such a scare,
What if it quarrels with his Grizzly Bear?

You still think you could keep your head?
What if the Lion from under the bed

And the four Ostriches that deposit
Their football eggs in his bedroom closet

And the Aardvark out of his bottom drawer

All danced out and joined in the Roar?

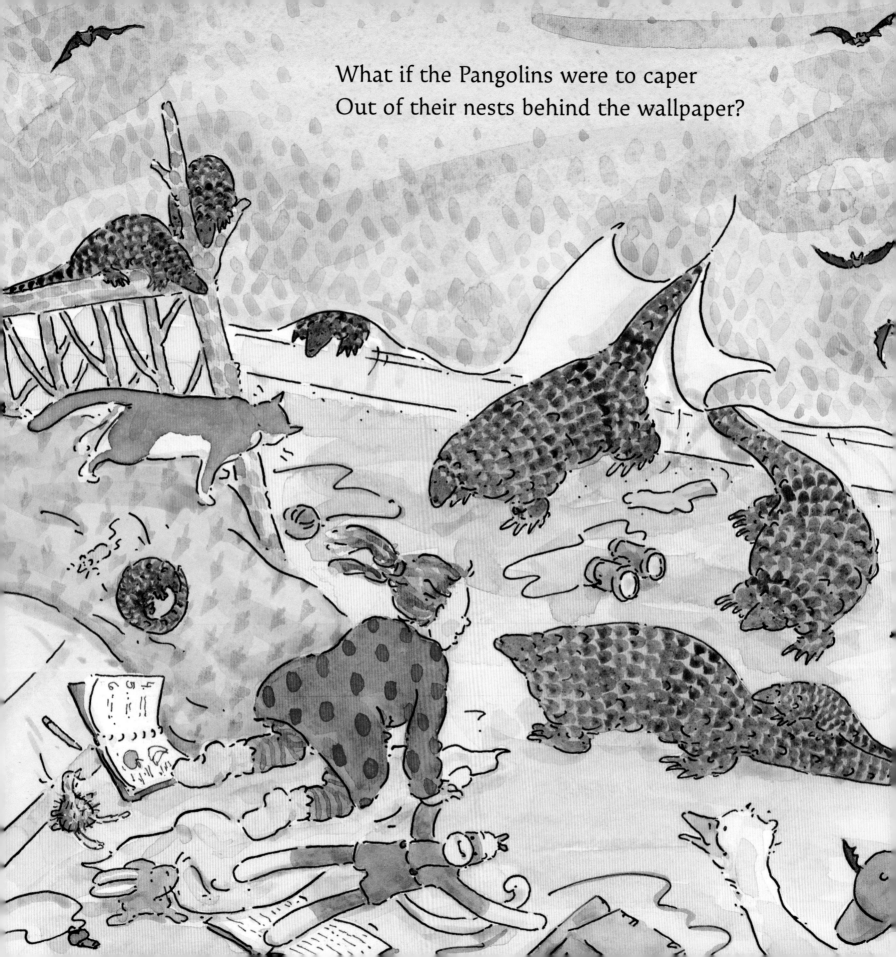

What if the Pangolins were to caper
Out of their nests behind the wallpaper?

With the fifty sorts of Bats
That hang on his hatstand like old hats,

And out of a shoebox the excitable Platypus
Along with the Ocelot or Jungle-Cattypus?

NO GIRLS ALLOWED!

The Wombat, the Dingo, the Gecko, the Grampus—

How they would shake the house with their Rumpus!

Not to forget the Bandicoot
Who would certainly peer from his battered old boot.

Why it could be a dreadful day,

And what Oh what would the neighbours say!

To my brothers Doug and Court
—T.C.P.

Text copyright © 2009 by the Estate of Ted Hughes
Pictures copyright © 2009 by Tracey Campbell Pearson
All rights reserved
Distributed in Canada by Douglas & McIntyre Ltd.
Color separations by Embassy Graphics
Printed and bound in the United States of America by Phoenix Color Corporation
Designed by Jonathan Bartlett
First edition, 2009
1  3  5  7  9  10  8  6  4  2

www.fsgkidsbooks.com

Library of Congress Cataloging-in-Publication Data
Hughes, Ted, 1930–1998.
    My brother Bert / Ted Hughes ; pictures by Tracey Campbell Pearson.— 1st ed.
        p.   cm.
    Summary: Illustrations and rhyming text portray a hobby gone awry, as Bert's collection of exotic
pets seems on the verge of breaking into a quarrel, and perhaps a rumpus, as well.
    ISBN-13: 978-0-374-39982-5
    ISBN-10: 0-374-39982-4
    [1. Animals—Fiction.   2. Pets—Fiction.   3. Hobbies—Fiction.   4. Stories in rhyme.]   I. Pearson, Tracey
Campbell, ill.   II. Title.

PZ8.3.H867 My 2009
[E]—dc22

                                                                                    2007034415

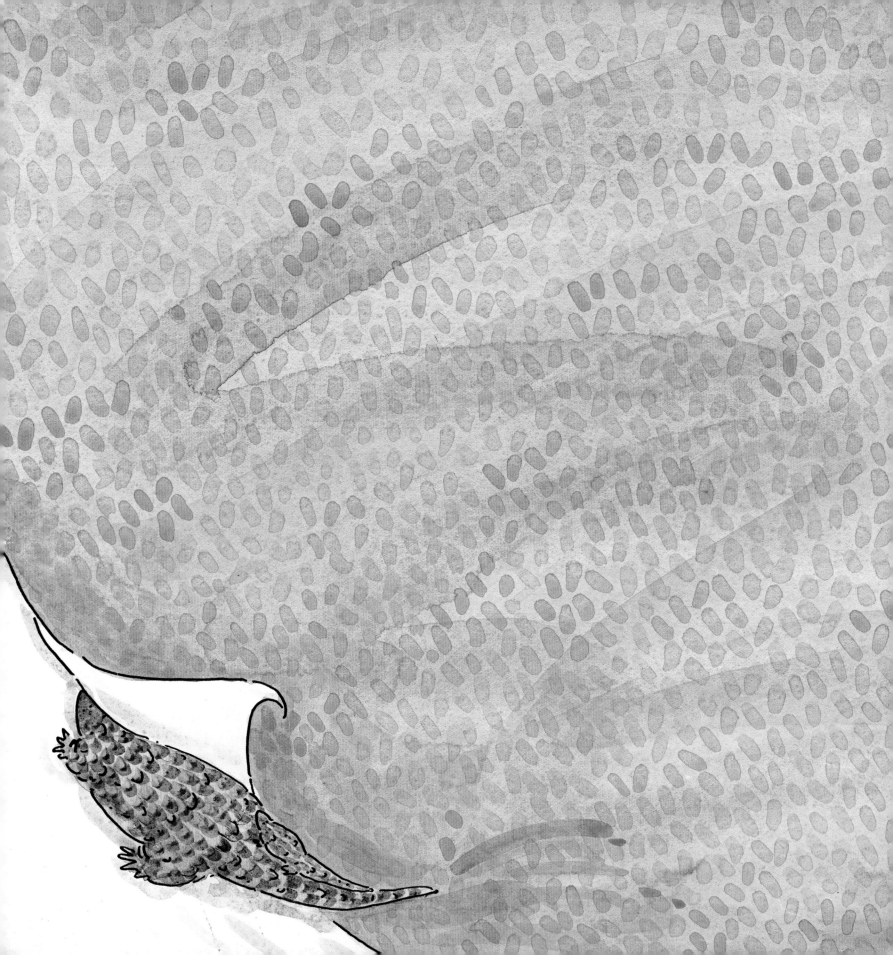